Aubrey Wenger

Poopoos Love Potties

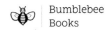 Bumblebee
Books

BUMBLEBEE PAPERBACK EDITION

A CIP catalogue record for this title is
available from the British Library.

ISBN: 978-1-83934-943-0

Bumblebee Books is an imprint of
Olympia Publishers.

First Published in 2024

Olympia Publishers
Tallis House
2 Tallis Street
London
EC4Y 0AB

Printed in Great Britain

Dedication

For Lola, Nora & Axel

So, you're working hard to
use the potty.

Each day you're learning to
listen to your body.

Going peepee, that's just fine!

But what about poopoos?

You're scared? OH MY!

Well, don't worry because here are some things you need to know that should make it easier to go.

Everyone is scared of their
poopoo at first.
You're talking to an expert,
mine are the worst!

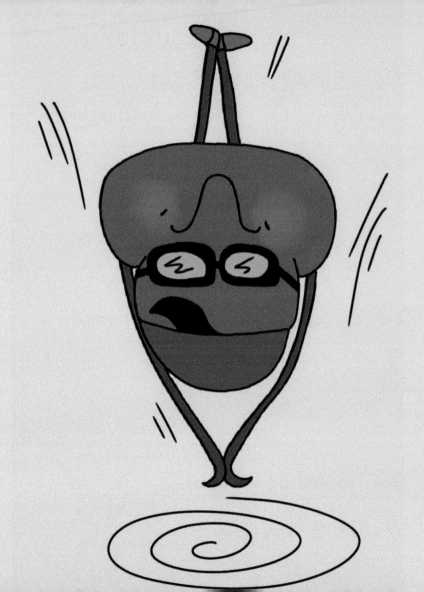

But the truth is, poopoos
aren't bad at all.
They just come out and
then they fall.

Your poopoos can't get you.
But they can be smelly.
It's just leftover food that
you put in your belly.

Poopoos love the potty
don't you see?
They just plop into the potty
and then they are free!

So next time that you feel that downward pressure,

read this story as a refresher.

Poopoos are normal,
everyone does it.
But big kids like you,
know what to do!

Now get that thing in the potty
where it wants to be,
because your poopoos
love the potty!

About the Author

Aubrey Wenger is a wife, mother of three, homemaker and birth doula. She is both proud and humbled by the experience of motherhood. She lives a simple life in Wisconsin where she has fun doing home projects with her husband and taking their children on outings together. Her hobbies include creating the occasional painting, cooking old family recipes and learning new skills.

Acknowledgements

Thank you to my daughter Nora, who without making potty-training so difficult, this story would never have been created.